OH BROTHER,
OH SISTER

OH BROTHER, OH SISTER

M. D. Hyman

authorHOUSE®

AuthorHouse™
1663 Liberty Drive
Bloomington, IN 47403
www.authorhouse.com
Phone: 1-800-839-8640

Published by AuthorHouse   02/29/2012

ISBN: 978-1-4685-5518-9 (sc)
ISBN: 978-1-4685-5517-2 (e)

Library of Congress Control Number: 2012903150

Contents

Part 1—Oh Brother

Part 2—Oh Sister

PART 1

OH BROTHER

PREFACE

Captain Dan McCroy and Lieutenant Linda Clark walked into the dining room of the Somerset Hills Hotel, hoping to find Janice Moore in there. Well, they found her alright. She was dead on the floor with a knife through her heart. It was not a pretty sight. Captain McCroy lowered his head out of respect for the victim and replied, "I'm sorry Miss Moore, if only we had gotten here sooner." Lieutenant Clark nodded in agreement. She felt as bad as he did.

CHAPTER 1

L AST NIGHT, A birthday party was held in honor of Tom Costa, in the dining room at the Somerset Hills Hotel. He had just turned 50 and had insisted on a fancy affair, since he was now officially a half-century old. Most people would have thought it ridiculous to waste a lot of money like that for a birthday. Then again, most people wouldn't mess with a retired mob leader either. Anyway, as Tom finished his birthday speech, he was about to take a sip from his champagne glass when he started to go into cardiac arrest. His personal doctor told his body guard, Rajan, to bring Tom's car to the back of the hotel and take him to the hospital, because an ambulance would cause too much attention. Captain McCroy, who was at Tom's party, noticed something very interesting. Even though Tom didn't drink any champagne before going into cardiac arrest, it contained an ingredient that he didn't expect to find. He dipped his pinky in the champagne, tasted it, and replied, "I should've known."

Lieutenant Clark was stunned when she heard what the captain had discovered. "Morphine? His champagne had morphine in it? Are you sure about that?"

"I tasted it myself." He replied, "It was definitely morphine."

Captain McCroy sat down in his chair, consumed with his thoughts.

Lieutenant Clark then said, "You do realize that if he hadn't started having chest pains, and had drunk the champagne, he would've died. Then we would be investigating a murder. Right now, this is considered an attempted murder."

"Yeah, like I didn't know that already." McCroy said, rolling his eyes. "It just doesn't make any sense. Tom's ten-year-old daughter, Jenny, was sitting on his right side next to his champagne class. His ex-wife, Carla, was sitting on his left side, away from the champagne glass. Sitting next to Carla was her best friend, Janice Moore. Carla had gotten up to use the restroom, and came back into the room just when Tom was having his heart attack."

"You didn't see a waiter refill his glass or anything?" asked Lieutenant Clark.

"It was a buffet, and there were bottles everywhere." said McCroy. "There were no waiters. Look, the only way we're going to get any straight answers is if we question his family. They were seated around him, maybe they noticed something."

"Captain," asked the lieutenant, "why were you at the party?"

He stared at her for a minute before he gave a response. "Isn't it obvious? I received an invitation. And when you receive an invitation from a retired mob leader, you don't say 'no'."

Adriana, the housekeeper, opened the door. "Ah Captain McCroy, buongiorno. How good of you to come."

"Buongiorno Adriana," said McCroy, politely. "How's the household today?"

"It is very upsetting here." said Adriana, shaking her head. "Poor Jenny has been spending so much time alone at the stables, and Signora Costa is in such a state of shock."

"Speak of the devil," said Lieutenant Clark, as Carla Costa herself came hurrying down the stairs appearing very anxious. Who wouldn't be anxious after seeing your ex-husband having a heart attack.

"Oh great, it's you," she said directly to McCroy, "what do you want?"

"There's been a development." McCroy said, in a serious tone.

"You two know each other?" asked Clark.

"Yes," said McCroy suddenly. He had forgotten that the lieutenant was standing right next to him. "We met at the party. Lieutenant Clark this is Ms. Carla Costa, Tom's ex-wife. Ms. Costa, this is my lieutenant. Now I understand that this is a difficult time for you," McCroy said calmly, "but I'm afraid there's been a discovery. Someone put a very large dose of morphine in Tom's champagne glass in an attempt to try and kill him."

Carla slumped down and sat at the foot of the steps, shocked and horrified. "I don't believe this. He had already taken a dose before he left. He shouldn't have needed another dose."

"Wait a minute," interrupted Clark. "He takes morphine on a regular basis?"

"It's for his heart." said Carla, now looking at the lieutenant. "His personal doctor prescribed it for him."

"Ms. Costa," said Clark, rubbing her forehead, "forgive me for mentioning this, but it is my understanding that you've been divorced with Tom for about a year now. According to the media, you had signed a prenup, which states that in the event of a divorce, you would get zilch in alimony. But after the divorce, if Tom were to die without remarrying, you would get everything: the house, expenses, even the condo you both own in Disneyworld. Is that correct?"

"We don't want to take up any more of your valuable time Ms. Costa." said McCroy, cutting in and glaring at Clark, "We would like to speak with Jenny. Where is she?"

"She's at the stables." Carla answered. "And tell your lieutenant to think before she decides to jump to outrageous conclusions!"

CHAPTER 2

"LINDA, WHAT THE hell was that?" said McCroy, demanding an explanation.

"What was what?" replied Clark, who was by now furious with the captain.

"That interrogation stunt you were trying to pull off in there! I told you she had left the room!" he said angrily.

"That doesn't mean we can exclude the fact that she has a good motive for wanting her ex-husband dead, Dan. Besides, she was only gone for a short time. She might have put the morphine in the drink before she left." Clark replied angrily. "Look at all the money she'd get. By the way, I'm getting pretty fed up with the fact that you're hiding something from me."

"What are you talking about?" McCroy asked in annoyance.

"Oh don't give me that B.S. Dan!" Clark shouted. "Your politeness towards the Italian? Your attitude towards the ex-wife and vice versa?"

"I told you. I got to know the family very well last night." said McCroy, exasperated.

"Oh yeah sure," retorted Clark, "you get an invitation to meet a mob family for the first time, and all of a sudden you get treated like you're part of their family, is that it?"

McCroy turned to face Clark, and was about to say something to her when a voice called out from inside the stables. It was Bella Ricci, Carla's sister. "Captain McCroy, I was wondering when you'd show up."

Both McCroy and Clark looked at Bella, then at each other. Finally, the two of them turned about-face and walked towards the stables in silence. McCroy finally spoke, "Ah, Mrs. Ricci, nice to see you again."

"Likewise I'm sure." she said politely. "Who is your friend?"

"This is Lieutenant Clark. Lieutenant, this is Bella Ricci, Ms. Costa's sister."

"Charmed," said Clark flatly, "where is Jenny?" As if she had heard the lieutenant, Jenny came galloping from the fields behind the stables and in through the open barn door. After Jenny got off her horse, Bella walked over to put the horse back into its stall. While she was doing this, McCroy decided to question Jenny and Clark decided to question Bella.

"Jenny," said McCroy, "I know that this is a difficult time for you right now, but I need to ask you some questions."

"Ok, shoot." said Jenny, which was Jenny's usual response when someone says they need to tell her something or ask her questions.

"Ok," said McCroy, "can you remember what was going on at the party before your father had his heart attack?" Jenny suddenly got teary-eyed at the mention of her father.

"It's not fair that Daddy had a heart attack." she said on the brink of tears, "He's always been so careful, Mommy said so."

McCroy realized that putting on an authoritarian look wasn't going to help get answers from an emotional ten-year-old, so he put on his nurturing look. "I know," he said softly, "that's why I need to know if something happened that might have upset your father, causing him to have his attack."

Jenny put on her thinking face and thought for a minute before she answered. "Well, nothing really bad was happening. Mommy got up to use the bathroom, and then Miss Moore slid into Mommy's seat. She was laughing and saying mushy things to Daddy. Then Daddy said some mushy stuff back to her. Mommy wouldn't have liked that."

"Oh no she wouldn't have," McCroy said in agreement. He remembered now that Tom and Miss Moore were flirting with each other after Carla had left the table. *It certainly didn't take him long to get over the divorce*, he thought. Jenny continued, "Meanwhile, Aunt Bella came up to our table, and Daddy and Miss Moore stopped what they were doing. Aunt Bella asked how everything was. We all said 'fine' and she told Daddy to try the champagne. He said he was saving it for his birthday speech."

"Really." said McCroy. "Your Aunt Bella told your father to try the champagne?"

"Oh yeah," said Jenny, "she was making a big deal about how it's the best champagne he'll ever have."

Suddenly, McCroy's cellphone rang. "Excuse me Jenny." he said. "Hello?"

"Hello, Captain McCroy? This is Janice Moore. We saw each other at the party last night." McCroy's eyes widened in surprise. He did not see this coming.

"Uh, yes, Miss Moore, I remember you from the party last night. What can I do for you?"

"There's something very important that I need to discuss with you. Can you meet me at the Somerset Hills Hotel in an hour?"

"Of course," said McCroy. Then the phone went dead.

While McCroy and Clark were walking back to their car, they discussed their separate conversations with the suspects. Clark went first.

"All I got out of Bella was that she's a horse lover, and she's a vet. She kept saying that it was terrible that Tom had a heart attack, but that she doesn't feel sorry for him. She claims that he treated Carla terribly and that he got what he deserved. I almost thought she was confessing to murder. But I forgot, Tom Costa had a heart attack, and is still alive."

"Jenny said Bella kept insisting that he drink the champagne, that it would be the best champagne he'll ever have."

"What did she mean by that? You don't think that she laced the champagne with morphine do you?"

"At this point I can't assume anything yet until after I talk to Miss Moore. She just called on my cell phone, and asked to see me at the Somerset Hills Hotel in an hour."

"An hour? But the hotel is not that far from the estate. What'll we do with all that time?"

"Well, on the way, we stop at the hospital and check in on our patient. Better yet, I'll go see Mr. Costa, you go to the cafeteria and grab us some lunch. I'm starving."

"Hospital food for lunch?"

"Hey, desperate times call for desperate measures. Besides, I'm hungry. I'll eat anything, even if it is hospital food."

CHAPTER 3

L IEUTENANT CLARK FELT like throwing up the sandwich she ate in the car, after seeing Janice Moore dead on the floor, with a knife through her heart. McCroy bent down to examine the body, and replied. "Oh no," he said in a serious tone.

"What is it?" asked Clark, trying very hard not to stare at the body.

"The body is still warm." He said getting up, reaching for his gun. "She must have just been killed before we walked in. Her killer might still be in the building."

"What makes you so sure?" asked Clark, nervously. She had left her gun in the glove compartment. She figured seeing Miss Moore would just be a social visit for the both of them, not a search for her killer.

Just then, who should appear from the double doors at the other end of the room, but Miss Moore's killer herself. Carla walked casually towards them with a smile on her face.

"Well captain, lieutenant, it seems that you won't have a chance to have that talk with my best friend. Or should I say my ex-best friend, since she decided to stab me in the back."

Clark chuckled nervously and replied, "I guess you decided to stab her back, literally."

McCroy steadied the gun directly at Carla. He started to piece everything together. "I guess you didn't take the news of your ex-husband's affair with Miss Moore very well," he said.

Carla now looked directly at the captain, and her smile transformed into a frown and she replied, "Do you think I was going to let that bastard have a blast after he divorced me? Hell no! Sure they tried to keep their relationship secret but I'm not stupid. All year I had to endure seeing the two of them flirting with each other. Pretty soon, their flirting turned into passion, and then they started talking about getting married."

Then McCroy said, "You couldn't stand to let that happen could you Carla. According to the prenup, you would get ziltch in alimony, everything if Tom died without remarrying, and nothing if Tom remarried. If he were to marry Janice, everything would go to her, even Jenny."

Tears were streaming down Carla's face. "Bad enough she had to watch me go through this year in this living nightmare," Carla shouted, "but one thing she was never going to see was her father marrying someone who isn't her mother! I would not let Jenny go through life with two mothers! I am her mother, and nothing and no one will ever change that!" She collapsed onto a chair while crying her eyes out. Clark and McCroy looked at each other for a few seconds. Then Clark asked McCroy, "If she killed Janice, who put the morphine in the champagne glass?"

Right on cue, Bella Ricci walked into the room from the double doors, holding a gun in her hand. "That was me," she said, now steadying her gun directly at Clark. Carla stopped crying, got up, and stood behind Bella. By now, McCroy's arm was weakening. He had been pointing the gun at Carla the entire time, but he had to keep stalling, he just had to. "Well, now I see how Carla beat us to Janice," McCroy said to Clark, "Bella must have overheard us talking about meeting Janice here in an hour." Now he turned his attention onto Bella. "Ok, I can understand why Carla would have wanted to kill Tom, but why you Bella? All because he divorced your sister a year ago?"

"Besides that," Bella shouted, now aiming her gun at the captain, "after the divorce, Tom started hitting on me! I was flattered at first, but I'm a married woman, and he didn't give a damn! The man's a pig. When there was talk of him marrying Janice, I wasn't going to stand for it. I told Carla that I'd take care of Tom once and for all. I arrived at the party before he, Carla, and Jenny showed up. I had already laced his glass with morphine. I poured champagne into his glass and placed the glass in front of his seat."

Suddenly, a thought struck Lieutenant Clark. "Of course," she said to McCroy, who by now had switched the gun to his other hand, "she's a vet, she has access to drugs." McCroy rolled his eyes in annoyance, he had figured that part out already. He was wondering how much longer he was going to have to stall when suddenly, the doors behind him swung open. Tom Costa had entered the room.

"Hey everybody, what's happening?" he said cheerfully, his gold tooth sparkled in his smile. Everyone turned and stared at him. Bella and Carla both fainted dead away, hitting their heads on the hard floor. Clark's knees buckled, trying very hard not to pass out. McCroy finally put his arm down and massaged it, looking angrily at Tom. "It's about time!" he retorted "Where the hell were you?!"

"Hey, hey, chill little bro. I wasn't going to let them shoot you. I mean come on, I had to get you some back up.

15

Unfortunately, we have a crowd brewing outside and I don't want the paparazzi shooting at me today. I'm not dressed for a photo-op." Clark looked from Tom Costa, to McCroy, and then back at Tom. *Well this one's for the books*, was all she thought.

Chapter 4

"THIS IS NICOLE Brown for News12 New Jersey. We have a breaking story in progress right now. Paramedics and police cars have gathered around the Somerset Hills Hotel and have just rushed inside the building. They are responding to an anonymous tip regarding a possible shooting inside the hotel. We go now to our live correspondent, Eva Lopez. Eva what's the situation like out there?"

"Well Nicole a huge crowd has gathered by the front door of the hotel. Police are trying to push back the crowd from blocking the entrance. Oh wait, here come the paramedics. It looks like there was a shooting after all!"

The paramedics were bringing out Bella on a stretcher. Her head was resting on a bag of ice. Eva pushed her way through the crowd and managed to get close enough to one of the paramedics in order to start asking him questions. "Excuse me sir. Is this woman dead?"

The paramedic looked at Eva and replied, "Far from it, the lady fainted and now has a concussion, all from trying to shoot at a couple of police officers.

"Why was she trying to shoot at police officers?" Eva pressed on.

"Look lady, I don't have time for this." said the paramedic, "I've gotta get this lady in the ambulance, and go back in the hotel to get another lady who fainted, and another lady who's actually dead, so move out of the way!"

Eva straightened herself up and looked back at the camera and replied, "Well, there you have it folks. Two women fainted in an attempt to try and harm our policemen, and there's a dead body in the mix. I'll have more details to follow in this breaking story."

Captain McCroy and Lieutenant Clark watched the excitement from the roof of the hotel as the paramedics brought out Bella Ricci, Carla Costa, and Janice Moore. Tom Costa was watching the scene with them, along with his body guard, Rajan.

"Man oh man," sighed Tom, "to think that they wanted to kill me. It's just too bad they got to Janice first. Poor Janice." McCroy looked up at Tom and said, "If you learned how to keep your hands to yourself, you wouldn't have been in this situation to begin with."

"Hey I can't help it," replied Tom in a sly grin. "Women love me, and I love them." Clark looked up at Tom and said, "You disgust me." Then she looked over at McCroy, "And as for you, I can't believe you never told me that you were his brother!"

McCroy looked at his lieutenant with a pained expression. "I was trying to protect you," he said, "if you had known, you would've been swimming with the fishes along with me." Rajan jumped in, "Yeah, swimming with the fishes." He chuckled.

"Alright, alright," said Tom, "enough small talk. Rajan, is everything all set?"

"Everything's been taken care of boss," said Rajan. "Jenny and Adriana are packed, the jet's tank has been filled, we're ready for Disneyworld. All we gotta do is wait for the crowd to die down."

"Good," said Tom relieved, "because I expect an uninterrupted vacation. And it'll do Jenny some good to get away for a while. But I'm not going on any roller coaster rides. If Jenny wants to, either you or Adriana go with her. I'm not puking my guts out like last time."

"Oh yeah," said Rajan remember the last time his boss was on a roller coaster ride, "remember when you went on space mountain? You were already not looking so great just as you were getting on the ride with Jenny."

"Hey Rajan, you wanna swim with the fishes or you wanna swim in the hotel pool?" asked Tom in annoyance. Rajan gulped and said, "I'm gonna go check to see that the coast is clear," and he started walking towards the elevator. Tom tipped his hat off to the two officers and said, "Well, I got a plane to catch."

McCroy looked at Tom and said, "Just remember that you owe me big time, and try not to get yourself killed while you're down there."

"Relax Danny," said Tom cheerfully, "first thing I'll do when I get down there is shoot you an email." He turned and winked at Clark, then headed towards the elevator. By now the crowd was scattering, and the sun was setting. It was just the captain and the lieutenant, looking out into the sunset. After a couple of minutes of silence, Clark said, "I still wish you had told me, I thought as partners we're supposed to trust each other."

McCroy turned to his partner and replied, "We are partners, and I'd trust you with my life. But there are just some things that are too painful and too weird to mention. Besides, I'm sure you've got secrets you haven't told me."

He has a point, thought Clark, especially since she wasn't planning to confide in him about her deepest, darkest secrets.

19

PART 2

OH SISTER

PREFACE

L INDA CLARK TOOK a moment to look herself over with her compact mirror. She hoped she didn't look too girly, but yet professional. She is a lieutenant after all. Today however, she was not going to act like Lieutenant Linda Clark, and give off the persona she normally does while on the job. Today, she is just going to be Linda Clark, a woman who has a good job, a good life, and a good family. Of course, *family* is the one thing that she has to straighten out first.

Linda closed her compact mirror, and stepped out of her car. She walked across the parking lot cool, calm and collected, and stepped inside the Café Metro in Denville, NJ. *Nice place*, Linda thought, *quiet but friendly*. She walked up to the host counter and said, "Excuse me, I'm here for a 1:00 reservation."

"Name?" asked the host.

Linda took a deep breath before saying, "Well, my name is Linda Clark, but the reservation should be under a Cheryl Newberry? For two?"

The host looked at the computer screen for a minute before saying, "Oh yes, here it is. Cheryl Newberry. You're the first to arrive. Would you like to be seated now or would you prefer to wait?"

Linda breathed a sigh of relief. *Oh good I'm first*, she thought, *I'm definitely going to need a moment.* "Yes, I would like to be seated now," she told the host.

She was shown to a table near the center of the room, the bread and butter was already out on the table. Immediately she took a piece of bread, and started smearing butter on it.

"Would you care for a menu or wine list?" asked the host.

"No thanks," said Linda, "I'll just start off with a glass of white zinfandel."

"Very good, Ms. Clark," said the host. "I'll have that brought out right away."

As he walked away, Linda was a little taken aback by the comment. *How'd he know I was a Ms.?*, she asked herself bitterly. Even though it's true that Linda is unmarried, this was not the time to dwell on the fact that she's over 30 and still single. Right now, she needed to focus, and get it together. She had so many questions and so many thoughts racing through her mind. But the most important question that she felt needed to be answered first, is if this Cheryl Newberry is really, and undeniably, related to her.

CHAPTER 5

C APTAIN DAN McCROY was driving and talking about the case that he and his partner, Lieutenant Linda Clark, had just solved. It was without a doubt, one of the most bizarre and short-lived cases he ever had in his whole career.

"I mean if only my brother just kept his hands to himself, none of this would have happened!" said McCroy. "I know he can be a real heartbreaker, but never did he, or I, ever think that his fooling around would lead to murder."

"Mmmm." said Linda. McCroy looked over at his partner, and it appeared that she was deep in thought and not really listening to him. He didn't blame her.

"Look Linda," said McCroy, "I know that you're still a little peeved that I didn't tell you about him, but honestly I never thought that my brother would ever come up in conversion. Hell, sometimes I even forget I have a brother, because that's how often I see him!"

Linda snapped out of her train of thought and replied, "What? Oh yeah. Umm, look Dan, don't worry about it. I understand why you didn't tell me. Honestly, I probably wouldn't have talked about my brother either if he were involved in the mob. That is, if I ever had a brother. But it seems like you two have managed to get along, despite your differences."

McCroy sighed and said, "Yeah, it wasn't easy at first. Believe me, I didn't want to have anything to do with him once he started getting involved in the criminal world. But after a while, he wanted to try and set better examples for Jenny, and keep a low profile from the media. Because of that, it made me realize that despite his lifestyle choices, he wants his daughter to have a good life. Also, it shows that he does not want her to follow him in his unlawful footsteps. So I check-in on them once and a while, just to make sure that he's keeping true to his word."

He pulled up in front of Linda's apartment complex. "Well, here's your stop," he said.

Before Linda could get out of the car, McCroy said, "Hey Linda, why don't you take a couple of days off. This case was a lot to deal with. Besides, you can use this time to go visit your dad to see how he's doing."

Linda thought about it for a minute before replying in a teasing manner, "You know, you're right. This case was a lot to deal with, and I need time to cope with the fact that you have a brother and you never told me about him."

McCroy groaned and rolled his eyes.

"But in all seriousness," Linda said, as she got out of the car. "I should probably go see my dad. It's been a while, and I know he'd really want me to visit him."

"Alright then, see you later." said McCroy.

"Good night, thanks for the ride." said Linda.

"Say hi to your dad for me." said McCroy, as he drove away.

"I will." replied Linda.

Linda was all set and ready for bed. She felt exhausted, but at the same time she didn't feel like going to sleep. She sat on her bed thinking that one case may be over, but a new one was just beginning. This time, it was a personal case, and she knew she wasn't going to get paid overtime for solving it.

She looked at the picture frame on her night stand, and her mom was smiling right back at her.

Linda picked up the frame and stared at the picture of her mom and said, "Oh mom, if only you were here to clear up this mess. I still don't think it's even true, but why didn't you tell me about this?"

Her mom had died only a few months ago, but Linda believed that she knew everything there was to know about her mother. *I guess parents never really tell their kids everything, no matter how old the kids are,* she thought. Linda wasn't really sure what to believe. She wasn't even sure if her father knew about what her mother had kept secret for so long. Hopefully, what Linda would find out from visiting her dad up in Rockaway, NJ, would be answers to her questions, instead of more questions that needed answers.

CHAPTER 6

LINDA DIDN'T GET much sleep that night. On the drive up to visit her father, she couldn't stop thinking about that dreaded call she received on her cellphone. It was only yesterday afternoon when she got the call. But to her, it felt like only minutes ago that she was talking to a complete stranger, who was claiming to be her sister.

Linda was trying to decide between purchasing a pastrami sandwich or a salad, in the hospital cafeteria. She knew she should get a salad, but time was of the essence. Usually she has to eat and run on the job, especially today. So she decided to go with a pastrami sandwich, and selected a ham sandwich for Captain McCroy. She had just finished paying for the sandwiches when her cellphone rang. She figured it was McCroy calling to tell her to hurry up, or an officer calling from the police station. But when she looked at the number that came up on the cellphone screen, it identified itself as an Unknown number. *This might be interesting*, she thought.

She flipped open her cellphone to answer it. "Hello," said Linda.

"Hi, my name is Cheryl Newberry, am I speaking with Linda Clark?" came the reply.

"Yes, this is she. May I ask what this is regarding?" Linda asked.

"Well, this is going to sound a little strange," said Cheryl. "You may want to sit down."

Linda was starting to get a little suspicious, especially since this person didn't sound like a distressed victim or a cop. She hoped that she wasn't dealing with a potential criminal.

"Ma'am, I don't think you realize this, but you are talking to a police officer, a lieutenant to be exact. So I would tread carefully right now if I were you." Linda warned her.

Cheryl took a deep breath, "I know who you are. But you don't know who I am. So, I'm calling to tell you that you are my sister."

"What!" exclaimed Linda. "Lady, you better start telling me what sort of game you're playing here, before I have this call traced and have you arrested for harassment! How did you even get this number?"

"Ms. Clark please," said Cheryl, "just hear me out. I'm not playing any games with you. I'm only telling you what you should know. I've been searching for a long time for some answers. And now, I finally feel like I may be getting close to those answers."

"Answers to what?" asked Linda, who by now was trying to calm down after hearing this woman claim that she is her sister. It didn't make any sense whatsoever.

"Answers to the questions that I haven't asked myself in years." Cheryl replied. "Such as 'Who are my mother and father?' and 'Why did they abandon me?'"

At this point, Linda was shocked and speechless. She wasn't sure if this conversation was really happening, but she didn't say anything. She wanted Cheryl to keep talking.

"You see, I am technically an orphan, since I was never adopted. I was bounced from foster home to foster home, until I was eighteen. None of the families I lived with really wanted me. And I didn't blame them, since I was a bit of a rebellious kid and teenager. By the time I finally aged out of the system, all I cared about was trying to make a better life for myself. A life I never received while I was growing up."

Linda felt a little bad for this woman, but was wary of how the conversation was going. She still owed Linda an explanation. "I'm sorry," said Linda. "I can't imagine going through what you've been through."

"Thank you." said Cheryl. "I appreciate that." There was a brief pause before she continued. "So, in order to start off my new life, I changed my last name to Newberry, because my old last name brought me nothing but grief. I managed to put myself through community college by waitressing and working at department stores. And now, I own a restaurant."

"That's great." said Linda, trying to remain calm and rational. "But it doesn't explain how we can possibly be related."

"Right," said Cheryl, taking another deep breath, "Well, here's the thing, I'm engaged. But before I get married, I need to finally put my past behind me. I've just been running away from it for so long. Now that I found someone who I love and want to spend the rest of my life with, I want to move on to the next phase of my life. But I can't do that, until I find out who my birth parents are, and why I was given up. I knew that I was born in Newark Beth Israel Hospital, so I figured that would be the first place to start looking for some answers. I asked the hospital to give me a copy of my birth certificate, and the person's name that appears as my birth mother, is a woman named Angie Phillips."

Linda almost fainted at the sound of her mother's name. *No,* she thought. *That's impossible.* Cheryl went on.

"My birth father's name is not on the birth certificate. I was told that usually means the father didn't want to be known, or that my birth was out of wedlock. I was also given the hospital form that was filled out at the time, and it said that Angie Phillips lived at 245 Lincoln Street in Summit, NJ."

Linda could feel her blood begin to boil, and her anger level was getting high. She couldn't believe that this woman was telling her all this.

"So I went to the address, and the people that currently live there told me that an Angie Phillips did use to live at that address. However, she and her family had moved to a neighboring town called Morristown."

Linda's heart skipped a beat. Morristown was where her mother's parents lived until they passed away. She would visit her grandparents' house there all the time as a kid. But before she could start telling this woman off, Linda heard another voice talking to her.

"Hey Clark!" shouted McCroy. "I've been looking all over for you? Who are you talking to? We gotta go!"

"Alright I'm coming!" yelled Linda. She had enough of this Cheryl Newberry anyway. She hung up her cellphone without so much as saying goodbye. This woman sounded like she was completely off her rocker. Although, Linda couldn't believe that this women knew that her mother's parents lived in Morristown. But Cheryl didn't know the whole address. Or did she?

Linda didn't want to think about it right now, especially if this was a prank phone call. She followed McCroy out of the cafeteria, carrying the sandwiches with her.

CHAPTER 7

L INDA PULLED UP to her parents' house in Rockaway. She wasn't sure how to bring up the subject to her father. She wasn't even sure if it was necessary to bring it up. It was possible that the whole thing was a complete joke. At least that's what Linda kept telling herself.

She knocked on the front door, and in two seconds her dad opened it.

"Hi sweetheart, good to see you!" he said, giving her a huge hug.

"Hey dad," Linda said, hugging her dad back.

"Well come on in you big celebrity. When were you going to tell me you were going to be on the news?" he asked.

"I'm on the news? Since when?" Linda asked.

"Since you and McCroy solved this case about a lover's quarrel involving the infamous Tom Costa." he said in awe. "I mean this story goes pretty deep in detail. I still can't believe that this all led to murder, over that thug! Cheri couldn't believe it either!"

Cheri was Linda's mom's best friend. They had known each other since they were in high school. Cheri checks in on Linda's dad from time to time. Good thing she does. Linda could tell that her dad seemed to be doing better. Linda didn't want to spoil the mood, but she had to get everything out in the open.

"Dad, I'm here because there's something I want to ask you. It's about mom."

Her dad whirled around to look at Linda and said, "Does this have anything to do with that Cheryl Newberry?"

"What!" exclaimed Linda. "She called here?"

"Yeah," he said, "and believe me, I thought this woman was taking me for ride with this story about how your mother is apparently her mother too."

"I can't believe this, how'd she even get the house number? I still don't even know how she got my cell number." said Linda, who by now was feeling exasperated and frustrated.

"Well here's what happened," Linda's father explained. "She called me yesterday, giving me her life story about how she was in the foster care system, was never adopted, and all that jazz. She finally got around to telling me she discovered that your mother and her folks moved from Summit to Morristown. Of course, I told her I knew that already."

"Wait a minute," said Linda, "Mom really used to live in Summit?"

"Oh yeah, your mom said that they couldn't afford to live in Summit anymore, so they moved to Morristown."

I guess mom never really told dad why, Linda thought.

"Did Cheryl tell you how she knew mom used to live in Summit?" asked Linda.

Linda's dad thought about it for a minute before saying, "Actually, she never told me how she found out."

Linda breathed a sigh of relief.

"So anyway," her dad continued, "this Cheryl person went on to say that she looked through the phone book, and there were three Phillips families living in Morristown. Of course when she called the "right" Phillips house, that was when she got the recording about how the Phillips no longer live at the address, and if anyone is interested in purchasing the house, that they should call the Clarks' at the following number. Then she called me."

"Well, at least that explains how she got a hold of you." Linda said. Her grandparents had been dead for about eight years. So her parents wanted to sell the house, but they couldn't find a buyer. Eventually, Linda's parents figured that the house would never be sold, but it was never taken off the market.

"So how did she lead into claiming that mom is her mom?" asked Linda.

"I said to her, 'Seems like you went through a lot of trouble, just to find out about the Phillips'.' Then she said to me, 'Well, that's because Angie Phillips is my birth mother.' I hadn't laughed so hard like that in a long time!"

"Dad! You laughed?" Linda asked, horrified.

"Well that whole story seemed like a pretty far stretch of the imagination. I mean, your mother was always a virgin, until she met me that is."

"Ugh . . . good to know dad," Linda said, looking annoyed.

"I said to this Cheryl person, 'Look, I appreciate the song and dance you put on, but if you're that interested in the house, talk to my daughter.' And I gave her your number."

Linda's head was swimming in a sea of thoughts. *Did dad really not take it that seriously that mom could have had a kid before they even met? And if that is what really happened, it would explain why mom, gram and pop, moved to Morristown.*

Then her father asked, "So when you spoke to this woman, did she say how much she'd be willing to pay for the house?"

Linda looked at her dad, and thought for a minute before saying, "No, we didn't really talk about a price."

Linda's dad went to the refrigerator to get a water bottle and said, "Well, don't lose her number, I wanna see if I can sell this house to her and be done with it."

"Dad, how can you stand there and talk about selling the house to someone who's claiming that my mother is her mother too?" Linda asked angrily.

"Oh please," Linda's dad scoffed. "The only reason why she would put that much effort into her story, would be to try and appease us, because she really wants this house. I don't blame her for going through that much effort, I mean it is a good, quality, American Foursquare."

Linda rolled her eyes. Her father can be totally oblivious at times, and not really see the real issue at hand. This was going to be one of those times.

"Alright dad, I'll talk to her again and see if she's still interested," she said.

"Thanks hun," he said, "Well, I'm gonna go food shopping for the week. I'll pick us up some steaks for dinner."

"Sounds delicious dad," said Linda.

"Well it's not often I get a chance to see you," said Linda's father. "You should do it more often."

"Yeah, when I'm not running around all the time catching killers," Linda teased.

CHAPTER 8

AFTER HER FATHER left the house, Linda sat in the kitchen thinking. It was possible that this woman was simply putting on an act, just to try and place an offer on a decent looking American Foursquare. But why bother coming up with an orphan story? And the details about where her mother had lived before she ever met her father, were too thorough. Suddenly, it dawned on Linda that there really was only one person who could clarify all this. Immediately, she went out through the kitchen door, and out the backyard gate. She then walked across the street, and made a right turn. After she walked all the way to the end of the sidewalk, she was standing in front of her destination. In front of her was a house she had been in so many times while growing up. Many happy occasions took place in this house, but today would not be a happy occasion. Linda was going to finally discover the truth about her mother's past. At least she hoped she would.

Linda took a deep breath, walked up the front steps, and rang the doorbell.

"I'm coming, I'm coming, just keep your shirt on!" came the response.

Linda had to laugh a little bit, since she hadn't heard that expression in a long while.

In a minute, the front door flew open, and out came a lavishly dressed woman. "Linda! This is an unexpected surprise!" she said smiling, giving Linda a very tight hug.

"Hi Cheri, it's good to see you too." Linda said, when she was released from the hug. "Listen, I can't thank you enough for checking in on dad. He seems to be coping very well."

"Well, death is inevitable. It's not something we can all run away from so readily." said Cheri. "So us old folks might as well live it up, and stick together, for as long as we got!"

"Hence the outfit?" Linda asked.

"Oh this? I just threw this on. I didn't feel like walking around in my jeans today." said a nonchalant Cheri. "So, you coming in? I want to hear about this case you were involved with that's all over the news."

"Well, I'm going to need a drink in order for you to get me to talk." Linda said teasingly.

"Oh great, you're in luck! I'm making cocktails." Cheri said, as she started walking down the hallway.

"Wow Cheri, way to live on the edge." Linda said, as she walked in and closed the door behind her.

Linda found Cheri by the bar in the sitting room, mixing the drinks. She sat down on one of the couches, thinking of how to start the conversation.

"So Cheri, besides being a good samaritan, what else have you been up to?"

"Well, there's not really much to do when you get to be my age," Cheri said, as she started pouring the drinks. "There's bingo night, volunteering at the nursing home, and trying to find something fun to do with people my own age who are still living." She brought the two glasses over, and she and Linda clinked glasses before taking a sip.

"That's not too bad," said Linda, "I wouldn't mind a bingo night every now and then. It would be a nice break, in-between catching bad guys."

"Well, that police department is lucky to have you." Cheri said.

"Speaking of luck," said Linda. "Dad got a call recently from this woman, who may be interested in buying gram and pop's house."

"Oh finally! That house has been out on the market for so long, you'd think everybody just forgot about it." Cheri said, as she took another sip.

"Yeah, so dad gave this woman my number so that she could call me to ask about a price. The funny thing is, when she called, she didn't ask me about the house. She called to tell me that she's apparently, my sister."

Cheri practically choked on her drink. "What!?"

"I know that's what I said! I figured this Cheryl person was trying to prank call me or something. And she said that all she wanted was to put the past behind her, by finding out who her birth parents are and why they didn't keep her. Then she went into very specific details about where mom had lived. I didn't even know mom used to live in Summit. Then Dad told me today that mom used to live there, but then mom, gram, and pop moved to Morristown to save money. But I don't buy it." Linda took another sip and then looked at Cheri, who by now was staring at Linda. "Tell me Cheri, am I losing it? Or is this woman really my sister?"

Cheri took a deep breath, got up from the couch, and went to the bar to pour herself another drink.

"Technically," Cheri said, very gravely. "if this Cheryl person told you all this, and has proof, then she's not your sister. She's your half-sister."

"She said the name listed as the mother on her birth certificate is Angie Phillips, and that an old hospital form had mom's address as 245 Lincoln Street in Summit." Linda confirmed.

"Well then congratulations darlin'," Cheri said, raising a glass to Linda, "you have a half-sister." And Cheri gulped down the whole drink.

"Cheri," Linda said, while rubbing her forehead. "How?"

"Not *how*." Cheri specified. "But *when*."

Cheri came back to the sofa and sat down with a sigh. "You know your mother and I were more than just best friends. We were like sisters. We did everything together, shared everything together, the whole nine yards."

"I know," Linda said softly.

"In high school," Cheri went on, "we felt like we had the whole world at our disposal. We knew we didn't want to become just housewives. We wanted to go to college and make something of ourselves. So we swore that we wouldn't get into serious dating, until we were at college together."

"Really, you guys were that serious about swearing off men?" Linda asked in disbelief.

"Hey kid," said Cheri, "one thing you've gotta remember is that it was the 60's. A time when women were starting to be regarded as more than just housewives. We wanted to be the first women in our families to go to college."

"So what happened?" Linda asked.

"Junior/Senior prom." Cheri said with such disgust, that she got up and poured herself a third drink. "We were seniors, just one month away from graduating high school. At that point, I had always stuck with the promise we made to each other, about not dating too seriously. Your mother, on the other hand, was a little bit flirtatious."

"Really? She was?" asked Linda with a bit of laugh.

"Well, she was just trying to be friendly. It's not like we never had fun while in high school. She just never went out on a date, alone, with any of the guys she attracted. If she wanted to go out with a guy who asked her out, it would always be a double-date, me and her, with the guy and some bloke that I'd get stuck with." Cheri said, as she took a sip of her third drink.

"So prom night." Linda prompted.

"Oh yes, prom night." Cheri said, coming back to the couch and sitting down. "We were laughing and dancing with our friends. Then who should show up but Larry Finkley. We had been on a double-date with him and some other guy, before prom. He had asked your mother to be his date for the prom, and your mom turned him down. So Larry went up to your mother, and asked her for a dance." Cheri gulped down the rest of her drink. "I said to your mom that I didn't think it was a good idea, that Larry seemed like bad news. But then your mom replied, 'Cheri it's just one dance, what harm can it do?' She had a point, it was just one dance."

There was a pause, and Cheri rubbed her eyes. "When the dance was over, it was time to eat dinner. I went to use the lady's room. When I came back to the table, your mom wasn't there. I knew she wasn't in the lady's room, because I was just in there. So I went looking for her. I was hoping she wasn't outside, but I knew I should check, just to make sure. I kept calling out for her, and no answer. I was starting to get a bad feeling. So I went over to the parking lot, praying I wouldn't find her there. Before I could start calling her name out again, I heard a car door slam. I ducked behind a car, and heard footsteps heading towards where I was. That's when I got a good look at Larry under the lamppost. He looked . . . happy."

"Oh, my, God," Linda said, horrified. She had to stand up. She couldn't look at Cheri. She put her hand on her mouth, trying not to break into a sob. Cheri kept talking.

"As soon as he went inside, I went up the row of cars, looking in each one of them. Finally, towards the end of the row, I found your mother, sobbing. No one, could have foreseen this, I didn't even think it would happen. I got her out of that car, took her over to her car, since we drove together. I told her to stay ducked by her car, and that I'd get our stuff. On the drive home, she made me promise not to say anything, until after graduation."

Linda turned around in shock, "Are you kidding me!" she shouted. "You just let that bastard get away with . . ."

"Hey!" retorted Cheri, "Remember, for a woman, it was important to get a high school diploma. If we had said anything to anyone, then it could have jeopardized your mother's chances of graduating from high school on time. Bad enough rumors were starting circulate about the aftermath of prom. So we couldn't risk talking about what had happened. And for some reason, Larry never even let it slip of what happened that night with your mother. Maybe because we didn't rat him out, he figured he wouldn't saying anything either. But believe me, he certainly was not going to get away with anything."

Cheri got up and went to pour herself a fourth drink. "After high school graduation, your mom and I knew we had to say something. Especially since your mom was about two months late. We both told your grandparents together, in the kitchen. We were expecting a loud and angry fight, after we finished telling them what happened. But instead, everyone was quiet, for about two to three minutes. Then your grandfather left the room, went into the den, and took the shotgun off the mantle."

Linda gasped, "What did pop do? Threaten Larry to marry mom, or he'd kill him?"

"Oh don't be ridiculous," Cheri said, taking a sip of her fourth drink. "Your grandfather was not the kind of man who wanted his daughter to get married right out of high school, especially if his daughter was going to be the first woman in the family to go to college. No, your grandfather just wanted to scare the bastard off, that's all."

Cheri and Linda both sat back down on the couch, and Cheri continued. "So apparently, when your grandfather went over to Larry's house to have it out with him, Larry had come out of his house, and was dressed in an army uniform. He had just stepped out of the front gate, when your grandfather pulled up to him in his car. Your grandfather asked if he was off to go join the army. And Larry had said, 'Yup, hoping I'll be able to get through training and still be able to go to Vietnam.' Your grandfather simply said, 'Well, I hope you do. Best of luck to you.'"

Linda burst out into a laugh, "You're kidding!"

"Nope," Cheri stated, "he let him go. Your grandfather figured that either he would get Larry for what he did to your mother, or the war would get him. And sure enough, a couple years later, Sergeant Larry Finkley came back to Jersey. He's buried at his parents' house in the backyard."

CHAPTER 9

L INDA AND CHERI were quiet for a bit. Linda was still a bit enraged with what happened. Her mother slept with this guy, against her will. *Probably a good thing the war killed him, and not pop*, Linda thought, as she finished her drink. She then got up to pour her second drink, and asked. "Why did gram and pop move to Morristown, if Larry was joining the army?"

"Because they didn't want to take a chance of him dropping by unexpectedly, and things getting out of hand. That's why your mom's Summit address was put down as the place of residence. In case he did come back, looking for her." Cheri said. "Besides, your mother had been accepted to College of Saint Elizabeth. So your parents figured that by moving to Morristown, your mom could commute easily. Sort of ruined the plan we had of spending our college years together at Sarah Lawrence. But we visited each other when we could. By Spring Break of freshman year, your mom had your half-sister, and named her after me, Cheryl."

It was the end of the story. Linda was now ninety percent sure that this Cheryl Newberry was her half-sister.

"I still cannot believe how clueless dad is about all this." Linda said.

"Your mother made me swear never to tell him. It was a part of her past she didn't want him finding out about." Cheri said.

"Yeah, but he would've understood." Linda said, as she came back with her drink and sat back down on the couch.

"It was her decision," Cheri said with finality.

"True, but now there's a problem." Linda pointed out. "What if this woman calls the house again? I don't think dad can handle all this."

"So you call her back, and ask to meet with her, someplace public." Cheri suggested. "Then find out what she wants. For all we know, she could just want some closure. She deserves at least that much."

Linda thought about everything she discovered that afternoon at Cheri's, back at her dad's house. It took a lot of courage for her mom to do what she did. *Hopefully, Cheryl will understand* Linda thought. She checked her dad's house phone; there were no missed calls or messages. Then when Linda went to check her cellphone, she realized that she forgot to turn her cellphone on.

"Uh, oh" Linda said to herself.

She had six missed calls, two were from McCroy and the other four were from Cheryl. There was a voicemail from Cheryl. Linda was tempted to ignore it, but she knew she shouldn't. She called her voice mailbox and listened to the following message, "Hi Linda, this is Cheryl. Look, I know I gave you a lot to think about the other day. But please believe me when I tell you that I'm only interested in finding the truth about my birth parents. That's all. I had spoken with your father, that's how I got your cell number. I got your dad's number after looking through the phonebook and . . . that's a whole other story. Anyway, your dad is under the impression that I'm interested in buying Angie's parents' house. Please be assured that I'm absolutely not interested in buying that house."

Linda laughed a little bit.

"All I want to do is talk, if that's alright with you. Can we try and meet up someplace? Please call me back."

Linda thought for about five minutes before making her decision. "If she really means what she says, then she deserves to have some closure." she said to herself.

Linda was waiting at their table in the Café Metro for about ten minutes. She tried rehearsing what she'd say to Cheryl, but the words weren't coming out right. Then she looked up at the entrance for a third time, and saw someone walking over to the host's counter. Linda had to rub her eyes a couple of times to be sure of who she was looking at. The host brought the person over to where Linda was and said, "Here you are Ms. Newberry."

"Thank you," she said, "can I get a glass of water please?"

"Certainly," said the host, "would you two like to have the menus now?"

"Uhh, I think we're going to need a minute or two." Cheryl said, taking a quick glance at Linda, who was looking at Cheryl with amazement.

"Very well," the host said, and then he left.

"Wow," was all Linda could say.

"Surprised?" Cheryl asked, with trepidation.

"Oh no . . . I mean I wasn't sure if you were going to make it or not." Linda said, quickly gulping down her white zinfandel.

"Yeah, sorry I'm late, I was at a fitting for my gown." Cheryl said.

Linda took a good look at Cheryl before commenting, "You look a lot like her."

"Really," Cheryl said, "I wasn't sure if I did."

"No I swear," Linda said, "I mean when you were over at that counter, I thought you were her. You have her hair, her eyes; your face looks a lot like hers. When I look at myself in the mirror every morning, I know that I got most of my looks from my father."

Cheryl laughed a little bit, "I'm glad." Then she quickly said, "That's not what I meant, I meant that . . ."

"No, no, I understand," Linda said, setting her glass back on the table and crossing her arms. "I guess you really are my mother's daughter."

"I guess," Cheryl said, rubbing her hands together. "but I highly doubt that your father is my father. I just didn't get that impression when I talked to him."

"Oh I believe you," Linda said, laughing a little bit. "He can really be unaware of things at times. Thanks for not pressing the issue with him about mom."

"No problem," Cheryl said, setting her hands in her lap. "I had a feeling he sounded like he didn't have a clue, and I didn't want to get him upset."

A waiter came to the table to fill Linda's water glass, and then left.

"So what was she like?" Cheryl asked.

"Well," said Linda "before we get into that. You should know what happened."

Linda told Cheryl everything that Cheri told Linda.

"Oh my God," Cheryl said, "that bastard!"

"I know!" Linda said.

"They should have gone to the police about it." Cheryl said, angrily.

"They should have." Linda agreed. "But maybe Cheri was right, that things could have gotten out of control. Maybe mom wouldn't have been able to graduate on time. Who knows?"

"Do you think? . . ." Cheryl hesitated, "Do you think that if mom had kept me, things would have still turned out the way that they did? Would she still have been able to go to college and marry your dad?"

Linda took a couple of minutes to think before replying, "I honestly couldn't say. But I think that she wanted to give herself, and you, a chance at a better life."

"Yeah and look how I turned out." Cheryl said, sardonically.

"Are you kidding me?" Linda said, "You made your way into the world on your own. Now you're your own boss at a restaurant, and getting married. I may have had a decent childhood, but I'm still single. You defeated the odds. I think that if mom were still alive, she'd be proud of you."

"Thanks," Cheryl said, a little flushed.

Linda raised her water glass, "I propose a toast. To our mother. She may have had to make some sacrifices in the past, but I know she's looking down at us, and she's happy to see us together. If she were sitting with us, I know she'd be proud to call us both, her daughters." Cheryl got a little misty-eyed, and raised her water glass, "To mom.", and they clinked glasses. A waiter came back to their table and asked, "Alright ladies, are we ready?" Linda and Cheryl looked at each other, and Linda said, "We're going to need some menus."

Cheryl said, "Yes, and we're going to need some more water and a wine list."

"Alright then," said the waiter, and he left.

Linda and Cheryl looked back at each other, and smiled. This was going to be the start of an unusual, but fascinating, sister relationship.

EPILOGUE

"SO LET ME get this straight," said Dan McCroy. "You have a sister, and now is when you decide to tell me?"

"Half-sister," Linda clarified, while driving and talking to McCroy through her bluetooth earpiece. "Listen, I just discovered all of this over the past couple of days, and I'm coming clean to you about it. You wouldn't come clean to me about your brother, until we had to deal with that case which involved him, and the whole family drama that came with it."

"Alright alright you win," said McCroy, giving in. "You're better at delivering life-altering news than I am. So now what?"

"Well, I'm on my way back," Linda replied. "I can't stay away from work forever. But pretty soon, I'm going to have to take a little more time off, because I'm moving."

"Moving? Moving where?" asked Dan.

"I'm going to move into my grandparents' house in Morristown." Linda said. "I might as well. I mean the mortgage has already been paid, and no one is interested in that house. Also, at least I won't be that far away from my dad, so I can visit him more often."

"Yeah, but the commute from there to work is going to be a killer," said Dan.

"I'll manage." said Linda.

"Now what about your sister? I mean half-sister?" Dan asked.

"Well, we're going to work on the relationship. I'm not saying that it'll be easy, but I think we're off to a good start." Linda said.

"What about your dad? When is he going to find out about this?" Dan asked.

Linda paused briefly before saying, "For now, what he doesn't know won't hurt him. But I think that Cheri will get a kick out of it when she meets Cheryl."

Dan sighed, "Well, I really hope that this works out for you. If you run into any sibling problems, I'm here for you."

"Thanks Dan, I'll see you soon." said Linda.

"See you at work." said Dan, and he hung up.

Linda breathed a sigh of relief. As she kept driving, she went over in her mind what had transpired on her visit. It was a lot to take in; finding out about her half-sister, and her mother's secret past. Plus, her dad still knows nothing about it. *How is this all going to work out?* she thought. Then she said to herself, "It won't be easy, but we'll make it work."

ABOUT THE AUTHOR

READING MYSTERIES AND watching them on TV will always be a part of my life. My mom is a fan of the ever so popular Mary Higgins Clark. She also enjoyed watching *Murder She Wrote, Columbo,* and *McMillan and Wife,* back in the day. So she didn't mind that I was exploring classic and modern mysteries while growing up in a small town in New Jersey. Of course I dabbled into Agatha Christie and Sir Arthur Conan Doyle. But a lot of my inspiration came from reading and watching modern mysteries, as well. Mystery authors whose works I have read, and grown to appreciate, are Sister Carol Anne O'Marie, Jill Churchill, Ann Waldron, Elizabeth Peters, Pamela Thomas-Graham, and the mastermind who created a post-life for Sherlock Holmes, Laurie R. King.

However, no homage to mysteries would be complete without mentioning the *Thin Man* series, *The Adventures of Sherlock Holmes,* and *Diagnosis Murder.* Also, let's not forget Midsomer Murders, Rosemary and Thyme, the Inspector Lynley series, and the now primetime shows Monk and Psych.

Printed in the United States
By Bookmasters